Ten Tales of
Brer Rabbit

Lynne Garner

Ten Tales of Brer Rabbit
Copyright © Lynne Garner 2017
Published by Mad Moment Media
www.madmomentmedia.com

Lynne Garner has asserted her right under the Copyright, Designs
and Patent Act 1988 to be identified as the author of this work.

ISBN 978-1-9996807-0-1

Mad Moment Media is a trading name of Nyrex Limited
Cover illustration and design by Debbie Knight

DEDICATION

For Mum, Valerie, Lily and Albert

CONTENTS

INTRODUCTION

I remember my introduction to the lovable rogue that is Brer Rabbit was the stories written by Enid Blyton (1897-1968). I also remember seeing the Disney film 'Song of the South' (first screened in 1946) which combined live action with animation. The film featured the award-winning song 'Zip-a-dee-doo-dah', which Brer Rabbit sang along to. Little did I know this film and Blyton's books were based on the Brer Rabbit stories written by Joel Chandler Harris (1845-1908), who in the late 19th century popularized this mischief-maker in his stories featuring Uncle Remus. I also didn't know that Joel Chandler Harris hadn't pulled Brer Rabbit from his own imagination, but had collected the stories and retold them.

Brer Rabbit tales were originally an oral tradition that had travelled the world with the thousands of people sold into slavery. Slaves and those descended from them tended not to share their stories with people outside their own circle. However, this changed in the late 1800s when people including Robert Barnhill Roosevelt (1829-1906), Alcée Fortier (1856-1914) and Joel Chandler Harris began to collect the stories and write them down. Although Robert

Barnhill Roosevelt published a small collection of Brer Rabbit stories before the Uncle Remus books, these didn't capture the public's imagination. It wasn't until Joel Chandler Harris published his books that Brer Rabbit became a popular trickster character, loved by thousands of readers.

The stories retold in this collection are based on those that appeared in the books written by Joel Chandler Harris. In his early twenties he worked on a plantation where he overheard stories being shared by the slaves - namely Uncle George Terrell, Old Harbert and Aunt Sissy. In order to keep the feel of the original stories (they were told in the Deep South Gullah dialect) he wrote them in what is called an 'eye dialect', the non-standard spelling of words used to mimic the original dialect.

Some of the stories he retold in his seven Uncle Remus books are very similar to other trickster stories, including those featuring Anansi the Trickster Spider. For example, in the story 'The Tar Baby' Brer Fox constructs a doll out of a lump of tar in the hopes of capturing Brer Rabbit. This story is very similar to the Anansi story featuring the gum doll created by the farmer in a bid to capture Anansi. Another story where Brer Rabbit manages to ride Brer Fox is very similar to the story where Anansi the Trickster Spider fools Tiger into allowing him to ride him. This mingling of stories would appear to support the theory held by some, that a few of the Brer Rabbit stories are a mixture of traditional African tales and stories told by the Native American Indians.

Typically in the stories featuring Brer Rabbit, he tricks the same characters repeatedly and they never learn that this rapscallion will outwit them. Whereas in the Anansi the Trickster Spider tales Anansi typically manages to fool someone just once and, unlike Brer Rabbit, sometimes becomes the victim of his own tricks.

Whether you've read a Brer Rabbit story before or not, I hope you enjoy them as much as I've enjoyed researching and writing them. Lastly, if these stories have kept you entertained then you may also like my retellings of some of the Anansi the Trickster Spider and Coyote stories available in printed format and as eBooks.

Lynne Garner, September 2017.

"There is little use building a fence around the garden to keep out the rabbits."

Yugoslavian proverb

BRER RABBIT AND THE VEGETABLE PATCH

The very old farmer had the best vegetable patch in the village. Well, he would, wouldn't he? He'd hoe, dig and water his carrots, radish and cucumbers every day. And every year the very old farmer won at least one prize at the fall fair for his vegetables. Sometimes he'd win two, three, even four prizes. If he wasn't looking after his vegetable patch he'd be looking after his three hound dogs, Blue, Black and Brown. Many wondered which he loved more, his vegetables or his old hound dogs.

Now Brer Rabbit often watched the very old farmer care for his vegetables from the safety of a large bush. He'd tried to get into the vegetable patch but he had never managed to. You see, the very old farmer was also good at making fences that kept rabbits out. He made them too tall for a rabbit to hop over; he made the gaps too small for even the smallest kitten to squeeze through. (Isn't it strange that a baby rabbit shares the same name as a baby cat?) He'd also pile large rocks around the inside of the fence so rabbits couldn't dig under it. Well, that changed one morning when Brer Rabbit noticed a loose nail.

"What have we got here?" Brer Rabbit asked himself, as he carefully pushed the slat in the fence to one side. "Just right for a rabbit to slip through."

He slipped through the gap and looked around. He couldn't believe his luck.

"Oh my!" he said. "Where to start?"

Brer Rabbit hopped over to the line of carrots and sniffed them. "Carrot tops, one of my favorites." He grabbed a carrot top and nibbled and nibbled until it came away from the carrot.

"Absolutely delicious," he said. "I think I'll take a couple of these home."

And with a nibble here and a nibble there Brer Rabbit soon had an armful of carrot tops. He then slipped back through the gap and hopped home.

•

The next morning the very old farmer visited his vegetable patch and as he closed the gate behind him, he noticed the carrot tops were missing.

"The cheek of it! Who's been at my carrots?" he asked himself. "Perhaps they've left me a clue."

Luckily for Brer Rabbit, just as the very old farmer reached the line of carrots, a gust of wind blew Brer Rabbit's footprints away. So try as he might, the very old farmer couldn't work out who'd taken his carrot tops.

•

That evening Brer Rabbit pulled back the loose fence panel and snuck into the vegetable patch.

"Mmm, what should I take tonight?" he asked himself.

He looked around and spotted a line of radish.

"Perhaps just a few of them," he said. And with a nibble here and a nibble there Brer Rabbit soon had an armful of radish tops. He then slipped out and hopped home to enjoy his feast.

•

The next morning the very old farmer visited his vegetable patch and as he closed the gate behind him, he noticed the radish tops were missing.

"The cheek of it! Now they've been at my radish," he said, shaking his head. "Perhaps they've left me a clue." Luckily for Brer Rabbit, just as the very old farmer reached the line of radish, a gust of wind blew Brer Rabbit's footprints away. So, try as he might, the very old farmer couldn't work out who'd taken his radish tops.

•

That evening Brer Rabbit pulled back the loose fence panel and snuck into the vegetable garden.

"Mmm, I fancy something different tonight. What shall I take?" He looked around and spotted a line of cucumbers.

"Perhaps just a few leaves from them and a few carrot tops." And with a nibble here and a nibble there Brer Rabbit soon had an armful of cucumber leaves and carrot tops. But as he nibbled there was the pitter-patter of raindrops.

"Better hurry," he said to himself. "I don't want to get too wet." He slipped back through the gap and hopped home to enjoy his feast.

•

The next morning the very old farmer visited his vegetable patch. As he closed the gate, he noticed more carrots tops were missing and some of his cucumbers were missing their leaves.

"The cheek of it! They've been in my vegetables again," he said, shaking his head. "Perhaps they've left me a clue." The very old farmer bent down and looked and what did he see? Some little rabbit footprints in the damp earth.

"So that's who's been visiting my vegetable patch," he said with a smile. "I think I should introduce that cheeky Brer Rabbit to my old friends, Blue, Black and Brown."

•

That evening as Brer Rabbit slipped into the vegetable patch he noticed something was different. He sniffed the air and heard a whimper and a whine.

"I know who that is. That's those old hound dogs," he said. "I'd better get out of here."

Brer Rabbit carefully hopped back to the gap, trying to make sure he wasn't noticed. But it was too late: Blue, Black and Brown could smell him.

"Go get that rascal, boys!" shouted the very old farmer, opening his front door. The three old hound dogs dashed out.

Brer Rabbit started to run. He wove in and out of the tree stumps and under the bushes. Soon he reached the road that led to his burrow. In the distance he could hear Blue, Black and Brown looking for his scent. They whimpered, whined and barked with excitement as they picked up his trail.

Just then who should Brer Rabbit bump into but Brer Raccoon, Brer Fox and Brer Bear?

Brer Rabbit had an idea. He ran up to them, then around and around.

"Hello, dear friends. How are you on this fine night?" Brer Rabbit asked between gasps.

He gave Brer Raccoon a big hug, then Brer Fox and finally Brer Bear, well at least, Brer Bear's legs. Now this hug wasn't just a little hug, it was a big hug, a best friend type of hug.

"I'm sorry," Brer Rabbit said. "I'm running late and I must dash but it would have been rude not to say hello."

Brer Rabbit then quickly hopped in the direction of his burrow, leaving three friends very confused.

"What was all that about?" asked Brer Raccoon.

"Not a clue," replied Brer Fox.

"Do you think it has anything to do with those hound dogs?" asked Brer Bear, pointing down the lane.

"I wouldn't…" said Brer Raccoon, but he didn't have time to finish his sentence because just then Blue, Black and Brown came into view.

Blue, Black and Brown stopped running and looked at each other, confused.

"None of them looks like Brer Rabbit," said Blue.

"But they all smell like Brer Rabbit," said Black.

"So, which one do we chase?" asked Brown.

The old hound dogs looked at one another, grinned and said, "ALL of them!"

"I'll chase the one on the left," said Blue.

"I'll chase the one in the middle," said Black.

"I'll chase the one on the right," said Brown.

As the three hounds decided which friend to chase the three friends looked at one another.

"I think they're going to chase us," said Brer Raccoon.

"I think you're right," said Brer Fox.

"We'd better run," said Brer Bear.

Blue, Black and Brown barked with excitement. "After them!"

The old hound dogs started to run and so did the three friends.

As he ran, Brer Raccoon looked over his shoulder and he saw to his dismay Blue getting nearer and nearer. Just as Blue was about to nip Brer Raccoon's tail he reached a tree and climbed it faster than he'd ever climbed a tree before.

Blue crashed into the tree with a large thump!

"I didn't know rabbits could do that," he said rubbing his head.

Suddenly Brer Raccoon knew why Brer Rabbit had hugged him so tightly. "That crafty old rabbit," he said. "He left his scent on me so those old hound dogs would chase me and not him. I'll have to get back at him for this."

Whilst Blue was chasing Brer Raccoon, Black was chasing Brer Fox. Unlike raccoons, foxes can't climb trees. So Brer Fox used his cunning to outwit the old hound dog and hid, crouching on a large rock on the riverbank. As he watched Black trying to find his scent he heard the old hound dog say, "I didn't know rabbits could just disappear like that."

Suddenly Brer Fox knew why Brer Rabbit had hugged him so tightly. "That crafty old rabbit," he said. "He left his scent on me so those old hound dogs would chase me and not him. I'll have to get back at him for this."

As Blue was pacing around the base of the tree and Black was trying to sniff out the disappearing rabbit, Brown was chasing Brer Bear.

Now Brer Bear knew the very old farmer's hound dogs didn't like water, so when he reached the river he jumped in and swam. As he swam he looked over his shoulder to see Brown sitting on the riverbank, confused. He then heard him say, "I didn't know rabbits could swim."

Suddenly Brer Bear knew why Brer Rabbit had hugged him so tightly. "That crafty old rabbit," he said. "He left his scent on me so those old hounds would chase me and not him. I'll have to get back at him for this."

And as this mayhem was going on Brer Rabbit nibbled on the last of the carrots and cucumber leaves. "Delicious!" he said with a smile.

• • •

"A sure friend is known when in difficulty."

Quintus Ennius (239BC – 169BC)

BRER RABBIT HELPS SISTER GOOSE

It was a warm sunny evening and Brer Rabbit had decided to take a stroll down to the river. Just as he reached the small path that led to the riverbank he spotted Brer Fox trying to hide in a bush.

"Good evening, friend," said Brer Rabbit, hopping over to Brer Fox. "How are you this fine evening?"

Brer Fox sighed and came out of his hiding place. "I'm well, thank you," he said.

"What brings you out on this fine evening?" Brer Rabbit asked.

Brer Fox looked around as if checking no one was watching. "Just out for a walk," said Brer Fox.

Just then Brer Rabbit heard Sister Goose's voice being carried on the gentle evening breeze. She was singing one of her favorite songs.

Brer Rabbit was sure he saw Brer Fox sniff the air and lick his lips.

"She has a lovely voice," said Brer Rabbit.

"Yes, she does," agreed Brer Fox.

"You know I have a soft spot for Sister Goose. She is perhaps the nicest goose I've ever met," said Brer Rabbit.

"I think I'll pop down to the riverbank for a chat. You're welcome to join me."

"That's a kind offer but I have things to do," said Brer Fox, and with that he slipped through the bush and was soon out of sight.

Brer Rabbit shook his head and scratched his hairy chin. "That Brer Fox is up to something," he said to himself. "No matter. I'm sure I'll work out what it is." Brer Rabbit then hopped along the path down to the riverbank where he found Sister Goose washing clothes and covered in soapsuds.

"Good evening," said Brer Rabbit. "And how's my favorite goose?"

"Dearie me you made me jump," said Sister Goose, her feathers ruffling. "Oh, bother," she said as her glasses fell off her beak and into the river.

"Let me get those for you," said Brer Rabbit as he paddled into the water. He bent down and picked up the glasses, shook them gently, then wiped them with his red spotted handkerchief. "There you go, good as new."

"Thank you," said Sister Goose, sliding her glasses back onto her beak. "I can't see a thing without these. My eyes are almost as bad as my hearing. One of the problems with getting old."

"I know what you mean," said Brer Rabbit.

"It's a worry, you know," said Sister Goose. "If I can't see or hear, I'll never know when Brer Fox or Brer Wolf is creeping up on me."

"Don't worry, you have plenty of friends who'll keep an

eye on you," said Brer Rabbit.

"I don't believe those stories I hear about you," said Sister Goose. "I know you have a good heart."

"You're too kind," said Brer Rabbit.

"It's the nights I worry about most," said Sister Goose. "I never know who'll creep up on me when I'm tucked in my bed."

"Why don't you sleep in the rafters?" asked Brer Rabbit.

"Honk, honk," laughed Sister Goose. "How do you expect an old lady to get into the rafters?"

Brer Rabbit thought for a while and scratched his chin. "Have you tried using a large bundle of washing as a sort of ladder?" he asked. "Then you'll easily get up into the rafters."

"I'd heard you're a clever rabbit," said Sister Goose.

"You're too kind," said Brer Rabbit, who secretly liked to hear good things about himself.

Sister Goose looked across the river. "That sun is getting low. I should make my way home."

"Let me help you," Brer Rabbit said. "I'm going that way."

Little did Sister Goose know the only reason Brer Rabbit was going the same way was because her house was near the very old farmer's vegetable patch.

"Now who's being too kind?" said Sister Goose.

•

Once Brer Rabbit dropped Sister Goose off at her house he hopped over to the vegetable patch and peeked through the fence. "Just a little nibble on a few carrot tops would be nice," Brer Rabbit said to himself.

As he looked around, Brer Rabbit noticed the very old farmer's three hound dogs sleeping on the porch. He also noticed Brer Fox hidden in the long grass and he looked as if he was watching the front door of Sister Goose's house.

"I'd better keep an eye on that rascal," said Brer Rabbit to himself, as he pulled back the loose piece of fence and sneaked under it. He then hopped over to the carrots and started to nibble on them.

"That was lovely," said Brer Rabbit as he swallowed the last carrot top. "I wonder what that rascal Brer Fox is up to. I think I'll check."

So Brer Rabbit took another peek to find out what Brer Fox was doing. Just as he reached the fence he saw Brer Fox had crept forward and was now at the very edge of the long grass. Brer Rabbit was sure he saw Brer Fox lick his lips and he was sure he was staring at someone.

"Brer Fox, what are you up to?" Brer Rabbit asked himself.

Brer Rabbit watched Brer Fox to work out who he was staring at. Brer Rabbit followed Brer Fox's gaze and was horrified to see he was staring at Sister Goose's open front door.

"Sister Goose, you are getting forgetful," said Brer Rabbit, shaking his head.

Just then Brer Fox started to creep slowly forward, following the line of the long grass until he'd reached the open door. Brer Fox looked around, stared at the sleeping hound dogs for a moment, then crept forward and pushed the door open.

Brer Rabbit held his breath.

Brer Fox crept in then slowly and quietly made his way over to the bed, which had a large Sister Goose-shaped lump in it.

Brer Rabbit held his breath. He looked at the open door, then at the sleeping hound dogs on the porch. "You're such a clever rabbit," Brer Rabbit said to himself, with a smile.

Just as Brer Fox was about to touch the lump Brer Rabbit grabbed hold of the loose piece of fence, pulled it back and let it go.

THUMP!

Brer Fox jumped and looked over his shoulder nervously.

Blue, Black and Brown, the three hound dogs, woke up. Blue sniffed the air. Black sniffed the air. Brown sniffed the air

"Fox," said Blue.

"Where?" asked Black.

"Just there," replied Brown, pointing at Brer Fox.

Brer Fox grabbed the goose-shaped lump and made a dash for the door.

Blue, Black and Brown jumped to their feet. They ran across the yard, barking excitedly.

Brer Fox ran out of the door towards the long grass. As he did a sock hit Blue in the face.

"What was that?" Blue barked.

Then a shirt flapped against Black's legs.

"What's happening?" Black howled.

Then a scarf wrapped around Brown's legs and he fell head over heels.

"What …?" Brown yelped.

By the time the three hounds had untangled themselves from the washing Brer Fox had disappeared into the long grass.

Brer Rabbit let out a sigh of relief and looked in the direction of Sister Goose's house. He was just in time to see her fly down from the rafters where she'd been sleeping.

"Thanks goodness," he said to himself. "Well, after all that excitement I think I'll hop along home."

But he didn't go unnoticed. As she peeked out of her door Sister Goose saw Brer Rabbit's white cottontail disappear into the long grass.

"That rabbit is a clever fellow," she said to herself as she closed her door.

• • •

"Hello Rabbit, it that you?"
"Let's pretend it isn't," said Rabbit,
"and see what happens."

A. A. Milne (1882 – 1956)

BRER RABBIT, BRER BEAR AND
THE FRUIT BUSH

It was fall and the trees were full of fruit and the bushes were full of berries. Now, as usual, Brer Rabbit was being nosey. So, when he saw some of the other animals chatting he made sure he could overhear them.

"Have you seen the berries on the bush by Brer Bear's house?" asked Sister Goose.

"I've heard they're the biggest berries you'll ever see," said Brer Raccoon.

"I've heard they're the sweetest berries you'll ever taste," said Sister Squirrel.

"I've heard no one knows how good they are because Brer Bear won't let anyone near his bush," said Sister Sparrow.

"I must get a taste of those berries," said Brer Rabbit to himself. "I think I'll go and try some now." So off he went to Brer Bear's house.

Just as he rounded the corner, Brer Rabbit couldn't believe his eyes.

"Oh my!" he said. "Brer Raccoon was right. They are the biggest berries I've ever seen. I wonder if they're the sweetest?"

Deciding to find out, Brer Rabbit look around. "No Brer Bear to stop me picking a couple of berries," he said. But just as his paw touched one of the juicy, shiny, round berries he felt a warm breath on the back of his neck.

"And what do you think you're doing, picking berries from my bush?" asked Brer Bear, towering over Brer Rabbit.

Brer Rabbit froze for a moment and gulped. Taking a long deep breath, he slowly turned around and smiled.

"My good friend, I was just going to taste one of these lovely berries. I've heard so much about them."

"Mmm," said Brer Bear, placing his paws on his hips. "So you think I've kept my berries safe from the frost during the spring, kept the insects away all summer and the birds this fall just for you and everyone else to eat, do you?"

"I'm so sorry," said Brer Rabbit. "I didn't know it was your bush."

"Well, it is," said Brer Bear firmly. "And I have no intention of sharing them with anyone."

"Oh, I do understand," said Brer Rabbit. "Please forgive me." Brer Rabbit then hopped out of harms way as quickly as he could. He knew it was never wise to make Brer Bear angry. He was known for having a very big roar and a very big paw, which could flatten a small rabbit with one swipe.

On his way home Brer Rabbit thought about how he could get to taste some of those berries. Just as he turned the handle on his front door he smiled and said to himself,

"You're such a clever rabbit. I'm sure with a little help from one of my friends, a tin of dry peas and some grass I'll be able to trick that Bear out of some of his berries."

•

The next morning Brer Rabbit began to put his plan into action by visiting Sister Goose.

As usual, Brer Rabbit found Sister Goose covered in soapsuds and washing clothes on the rocks by the river.

"Hello there!" shouted Brer Rabbit. "How are you this fine day?"

Sister Goose flicked the soapsuds off her wings and smiled. "Hello," she said. "What brings you to my part of the river?"

"I'm here to ask for your help," replied Brer Rabbit.

Sister Goose smiled and said, "After saving me from Brer Fox, how could I say no? What do you want me to do?"

"Just a simple little thing," said Brer Rabbit. "This afternoon I need you to hide in the long grass by Brer Bear's house. When you see me drop my handkerchief I need you to rattle this tin and rustle the long grass."

Sister Goose smiled. "You're up to your old tricks, aren't you?" she said.

Brer Rabbit laughed. "You know me too well, my friend."

Sister Goose took the tin full of beans and Brer Rabbit left her to her washing.

•

A little later Sister Goose was hidden in the long grass

holding the tin. As she peeked out she saw Brer Bear coming out of his house carrying a small bowl. Soon he was counting, "One for me and one for the bowl."

Just then Sister Goose saw Brer Rabbit hopping along the small path carrying a long piece of rope. Pretending to be in a hurry, Brer Rabbit bumped into Brer Bear, knocking the bowl of juicy ripe berries out of his paws.

"Wh…" shouted Brer Bear.

"I'm so sorry," said Brer Rabbit. "I've heard a huge storm is coming and it's blowing everything away."

Brer Bear laughed, then said, "I haven't heard about a storm."

"Haven't you?" asked Brer Rabbit. "I heard it's ripping up fences, flattening trees and pulling up bushes."

Brer Bear looked up. "There's not a cloud in the sky."

"It's on its way," said Brer Rabbit. "I'm off to tie everything down, then I'm going to hide in my burrow."

"But…" said Brer Bear, looking confused.

Just then Brer Rabbit pulled out his red spotted handkerchief, wiped his face and dropped the handkerchief on the ground.

Sister Goose saw this and started to rattle the tin and shake the long grass as hard as she could.

"Oh, no! Hear that?" asked Brer Rabbit. "The storm is getting nearer. I must go and so should you."

"But if I leave my bush everyone will take my berries," said Brer Bear.

"I could tie you to that tree," said Brer Rabbit, pointing to the large old oak tree by the side of the bush. "Then no one will dare eat your berries."

"What a good idea," said Brer Bear.

"Quickly then," said Brer Rabbit. "I have my own things to tie down."

Brer Bear walked over to the tree and put his back against it. Brer Rabbit took the end of the rope and tied it around Brer Bear's feet. He then hopped around and around the tree winding the rope around Brer Bear.

"Not so tight," Brer Bear complained. "I can hardly breathe."

"It has to be tight, otherwise you'll get blown away," said Brer Rabbit, as he tied the other end of the rope into the biggest knot you've ever seen.

Brer Rabbit hopped back and looked at Brer Bear.

"Why are you smiling?" asked Brer Bear.

Brer Rabbit picked up the small bowl Brer Bear had dropped and hopped over to the bush.

"What are you doing?" growled Brer Bear, wriggling to get free.

"One for me and one for the bowl," said Brer Rabbit popping a juicy berry into his mouth. "Oh, everyone was right: these are the biggest, juiciest, sweetest berries I've ever eaten."

• • •

"The future is a trickster rabbit, full of surprise. Only the past is predictable."

James Howe (1948 – present)

BRER RABBIT AND THE POT OF HONEY

Brer Rabbit was enjoying a little nibble on some fresh, lush grass when he heard voices.

"I wonder who that is," he said as he lifted his head. Who should he see enjoying a walk along the path but Brer Bear, Brer Fox and Brer Raccoon.

"I'd better hide," he said to himself. "I'm not sure they've forgiven me for the trick with the old farmer's hounds." So, Brer Rabbit slipped under the hedge and was soon out of sight.

As they got nearer Brer Rabbit heard Brer Bear say, "I think that Brer Rabbit needs to be taught a lesson and I know just what I'm going to do."

"I'm happy to help trick that rascal of a rabbit," said Brer Raccoon.

"Me too," said Brer Fox.

"Then meet me by the old oak tree tomorrow evening and I'll share my plan with you. I've written it on a piece of paper and listed everything we'll need," Brer Bear told them.

"I'll be there," said Brer Fox.

"I'll see you tomorrow," said Brer Raccoon.

The three friends then went their separate ways.

From his hiding place Brer Rabbit smiled to himself. "So you plan to trick me, do you?" he whispered. "Well, now I know, I'll make sure I'm ready for you. All I need is to see that piece of paper."

•

Early the next morning Brer Rabbit hid near Brer Bear's house waiting for him to go out.

Brer Rabbit waited and waited. "Brer Bear, you must be going out soon," he said with a sigh.

Just then Brer Bear's door opened and out he strolled carrying a small wooden bowl. He yawned and scratched his head as he wandered over to his much loved fruit bush.

"One for me and one for the bowl," said Brer Bear, as he popped a berry into his mouth. "Delicious."

When the bowl was full Brer Bear slowly walked back into his house.

Brer Rabbit continued to wait. "Come on, my friend, when are you going out?" Brer Rabbit wiggled to get some feeling back in to his cottontail.

Brer Rabbit waited and waited. He was just about to give up when Brer Bear came out wearing his best fishing hat and carrying his fishing rod.

"About time," said Brer Rabbit, hopping from one foot to the other. Brer Rabbit then watched Brer Bear slowly amble along the path and down to the river.

Brer Rabbit smiled and crept out from his hiding place. "Wonderful! Brer Bear will be down at the river for hours. That'll give me plenty of time to look for his plan."

Brer Rabbit quickly hopped over to Brer Bear's door and gave it a push. It creaked open and Brer Rabbit hopped inside and carefully closed it behind him.

Brer Rabbit looked around. "What a neat bear you are," he said, impressed at how tidy Bear's house was.

"Now where would you leave such an important list?" Brer Rabbit asked himself, looking around.

Brer Rabbit started to search for the plan. He looked high, he looked low, he looked under things and he looked on top of things.

He finally stood in the middle of the kitchen and looked up. "The only place I've not looked is in those pots on that high shelf," he said. "I suppose I'd better look in there."

So, Brer Rabbit pulled a chair across the floor and put it under the shelf. He hopped up and stretched as far as he could. "Almost there," he told himself as his paws touched the smallest pot.

He took it down and carefully opened the lid. "Biscuits," he said, a little disappointed.

Brer Rabbit put the pot back, then he reached as high as he could and carefully took the second pot down. He opened the lid and looked inside. "Nuts, just nuts," he said, frustrated he still hadn't found Brer Bear's plan.

Brer Rabbit put the pot back. He then reached as far as he could and just as he thought he had hold of the third pot it slipped from his paw and landed on his head. "What…" he said. Then he felt something cool and sticky trickle along his ears, down his face and over his shoulders.

"Yuck, this is sticky," muttered Brer Rabbit.

Brer Rabbit tried and tried to rub the honey out of his fur, but the more he rubbed, the worse it got. "I'd better get out of here," he said.

When he got outside some of the honey ran into his eyes and he stumbled across the grass and fell into a pile of leaves.

"Bother, bother, bother," he muttered as he tried to get up. Brer Rabbit was now covered in honey and leaves.

Just then Brer Rabbit heard whistling.

"Who can that be?" he wondered, as he managed to stand up.

To his horror, Brer Rabbit saw Brer Bear. Rubbing honey and leaves out of his eyes, Brer Rabbit looked around for somewhere to hide but he was too late Brer Bear saw him.

"Who, who are you?" asked Brer Bear, his voice quivering.

Brer Rabbit realized Brer Bear was scared.

"I can have some fun here," Brer Rabbit thought. So he started to wave his arms and as he did the leaves rustled, making the strangest noise.

"Please, please don't hurt me," Brer Bear said, in a hushed voice.

"I'm not here to hurt you, Brer Bear," said Brer Rabbit. "I've been sent by Will-o'-the-wisp to warn you."

"Will-o'-the-wisp?" asked Brer Bear. "What have I done to upset them?"

You see, all the creatures knew about Will-o'-the-wisp and that you should never cross them. If you did, they'd trick you into taking the wrong turn as you walked home at night. If you were lucky you just became lost, but if you were unlucky they led you into danger.

"They overheard you planning to trick Brer Rabbit," said Brer Rabbit, using the most frightening voice he could. "They don't want you to; they like him."

"But… but," Brer Bear said, trying to explain that all the friends wanted to do was repay Brer Rabbit for the tricks he'd played on them.

"Listen," said Brer Rabbit. "You're very lucky they sent me to warn you. Simply tell Brer Fox and Brer Raccoon you've changed your mind and the Will-o'-the-wisp will leave you alone."

"It will?" asked Brer Bear.

"Yes," said Brer Rabbit. "But only if you promise to tell Brer Fox and Brer Raccoon you've changed your mind."

"I will," said Brer Bear, with a large sigh of relief.

"Good," said Brer Rabbit. "I'll go and tell them now. They'll be very pleased."

"Thank you, thank you," said Brer Bear, as he watched Brer Rabbit disappear into the woods.

Once he was out of sight, Brer Rabbit laughed and laughed until he was almost crying.

"What a clever rabbit you are," he said to himself. Then he looked down and saw he was still covered in honey and leaves. "Mmm, now how do I get out of this mess?"

• • •

"I would challenge you to a battle of wits,
but I can see you are unarmed."

William Shakespeare (1564 – 1616)

BRER RABBIT, BRER OTTER AND THE FISH

"This is the life," said Brer Rabbit, watching the sunset over the river. Suddenly he saw something move in the water. It was Brer Otter swimming among the reeds. "Hello there, Brer Otter!" he shouted. "How are you this fine evening?"

Brer Otter swam over, climbed out of the water and shook himself dry.

Brer Otter sighed. "Not good, my friend, not good."

"What's the matter?" asked Brer Rabbit.

"I've spent all afternoon chasing fish and haven't caught a thing," replied Brer Otter. "Now I have nothing for tea."

"Surely catching fish isn't that difficult?" Brer Rabbit said.

"I wish that were true," said Brer Otter. "Fish can be very tricky and so, so slippery."

"I'm sure I could catch fish," said Brer Rabbit.

Brer Otter laughed. "If I can't catch fish with my lovely webbed feet, then how are you going to catch fish with your small furry feet?"

"I'm sure I can," said Brer Rabbit. Then as he thought he scratched his chin and ran his paw slowly along the length of his left ear.

"I know," he said. "Let's have a competition. Who can catch the most fish in a morning."

Brer Otter looked at Brer Rabbit, he was sure Rabbit was up to his old tricks. "What's the prize?" he asked.

Again Brer Rabbit scratched his chin and ran his paw along the length of his other ear.

"If I win, you'll help me when I need your help, no questions asked. If you win, I'll help you when you need me," said Brer Rabbit.

"I'm not sure…" said Brer Otter. He knew how Brer Rabbit loved to play tricks.

"Afraid you'll lose?" asked Brer Rabbit.

"I'm sure I'll regret this but I accept your challenge," said Brer Otter.

"Wonderful. We'll meet here tomorrow at mid-day and show each other how many fish we've caught," said Brer Rabbit.

"I'll see you tomorrow then," said Brer Otter as he slipped back into the water. Brer Rabbit smiled to himself, stretched, got up and made his way to the port road.

"There you are, my old friend," said Brer Rabbit, when he saw the old fisherman rumbling along the road in his cart. "To put my plan into action I need to look the part." So Brer Rabbit rolled in the dust and then poked leaves into his fur. "That'll do," he said.

Brer Rabbit lay on the edge of the road, hung his tongue out and closed his eyes. He didn't have long to wait for the old fisherman to trundle past.

"Whoa there, fella," said the old fisherman, pulling on the reins. "What do we have here? Some poor ol' rabbit's been hit by a cart. Pity for him, but he'll cook up just right for my tea."

Brer Rabbit heard a thud as the old fisherman jumped down from his cart. Brer Rabbit felt a tug on his ears as the old fisherman picked him up. Brer Rabbit wrinkled his nose, as he smelt fish. Brer Rabbit felt the old fisherman put him gently in the back of the cart. Soon the old fisherman was on his way again.

Brer Rabbit opened an eye and to his delight saw fish upon fish upon fish. Slowly he moved his head to make sure the old fisherman was looking the other way.

"Wonderful," he said. "Now to put the next part of my plan into action."

Brer Rabbit silently sat up and pulled the catch out of the flap on the back of the cart. With a little bump, it dropped down. Brer Rabbit slipped a fish over the side and dropped it onto the road. He slipped another then another and another over the side and onto the road. When Brer Rabbit was happy with the number of fish he'd dropped, he carefully slipped over the side and plopped onto the road.

He watched as the old fisherman continued on his way with no idea what had happened in the back of his cart.

Brer Rabbit looked back along the road and rubbed his paws together as he saw the trail of fish. "You're such a clever rabbit," he said.

•

The next morning Brer Rabbit woke up early, ate breakfast,

then put the fish he'd taken from the old fisherman's cart into a large wicker basket.

"Now where's my knife?" he asked himself as he opened drawer after drawer. "I need to clean these fish down by the river."

After hunting around, Brer Rabbit found his knife and put it in the wicker basket with the fish. He then found his fishing rod and hat, dusted them off (he'd not used them for a very long time) and set off to the riverbank.

When he got there Brer Otter was nowhere to be seen. "I might as well start cleaning these fish," he said, getting out the knife.

He'd just cleaned the last one when he saw Brer Otter swimming towards him.

"Hello, my dear friend," he said, standing up. "What a fine day it's turning out to be."

"It is?" asked Brer Otter, as he came out of the water carrying three fish. Brer Otter saw the pile of cleaned fish gleaming in the sun.

Brer Rabbit saw the look of surprise on Brer Otter's face and smiled. "As I said, it's turning out to be a fine day."

"How did you catch so many fish?" asked Brer Otter. "I've spent all morning fishing and only caught these."

"And what wonderful specimens they are," said Brer Rabbit.

"Did you catch all these fish by yourself?" asked Brer Otter.

"Oh yes," replied Brer Rabbit. "My fishing rod may look old but it knows how to catch a fish."

"How?" asked Brer Otter. "What's your secret?"

"Oh, no secret," said Brer Rabbit. "It was like they were lying in front of me and I just had to pick them up."

"Well, it's clear who's won the competition," said Brer Otter, holding out his paw.

Brer Rabbit shook Brer Otter's paw. "And as I have more fish than I can eat, please take half," said Brer Rabbit.

"I couldn't," said Brer Otter.

"I insist," said Brer Rabbit.

"Thank you," said Brer Otter, who began to worry about the help Brer Rabbit would ask him for.

"I hope you enjoy them," said Brer Rabbit, who then thought, perhaps I'll play this trick on Sister Heron and Sister Mink. I never know when I'll need someone's help.

• • •

"Lazy foke's stummocks don't git tired."

Joel Chandler Harris (1848 – 1908)

BRER RABBIT, BRER TURTLE AND THE PIMMERLY PLUMS

It was a wonderful fall evening. Brer Rabbit and Brer Turtle were sitting under a tree by Turtle's pond, sharing some pimmerly plums.

"Thank you, my dear friend," said Brer Rabbit, as he popped the last piece of pimmerly plum into his mouth. "Those were absolutely delicious."

"They were, weren't they?" agreed Brer Turtle. "A pity these are the last ones."

"Especially as they're so difficult to find," said Brer Rabbit.

Brer Turtle smiled then said, "That reminds me of a trick I played on Brer Fox."

"I'd love to hear it," said Brer Rabbit.

Brer Turtle cleared his throat, wriggled a little to get comfortable and began his story.

•

It was last fall and I was enjoying an evening walk. I'd made it to the crossroads and was taking a little breather. Now it had been a very hot day and I was tired, so I decided to take a little nap. That is one of the benefits of taking my home everywhere with me. So, I snuggled into the long grass under a tree, tucked myself in and closed my eyes. I was in the middle of a lovely dream about chasing tadpoles in my pond when I felt a soft tap on my shell. As I slowly opened one eye I felt another tap. Then to my amazement the world started to spin. I opened my eyes and I saw four furry red feet. I knew who they belonged to, our dear old friend Brer Fox.

"Please stop!" I shouted. "I'm getting dizzy."

But the world kept spinning.

"Please, please stop!" I shouted as loudly as I could. "I'm getting very, very dizzy."

Just as quickly as my world started to spin, it stopped.

"You're awake," said Brer Fox, with a smile.

"I am now," I replied, annoyed that Brer Fox had woken me up. It was then I had an idea and decided to play a trick on him.

"I know why you made me dizzy," I said. "You wanted to stop me from catching some pimmerly plums."

"You catch something? I'd like to see that," said Brer Fox with a smile. "You're far too slow and clumsy to catch anything."

"I may be slow on land but you've never seen me underwater," I replied. "And you don't have to be fast to catch pimmerly plums. You just have to be patient."

"Do you really know where to find pimmerly plums?" asked Brer Fox, his mouth watering at the thought of eating one of the most delicious plums in the world.

"Of course I do," I replied. "There's a lot this old turtle

knows."

"Please tell me where I can find some," he asked. "I just love pimmerly plums."

"If I tell you, you'll tell everyone else where to find them and then there'll be none for me," I replied.

"I promise I won't tell anyone," said Brer Fox.

"I'm not sure," I said.

"Please, please tell me. I promise I won't tell anyone," pleaded Brer Fox.

"I'll tell you where to find some pimmerly plums only if you make me a promise," I said.

"What, what?" asked Brer Fox, eager to find out where he could find some pimmerly plums.

"I'll tell you as long as you promise never to tell anyone else and never to make me dizzy again," I said.

"I promise, I promise," said Brer Fox.

I pretended to think about telling him, then finally said, "OK, I'll tell you."

Brer Fox moved a little closer to me and licked his lips.

"Well, you don't have to go far," I said. "Just look up. They're right above your head."

Brer Fox looked up, looked at me, then looked confused.

"They're up there just waiting to be eaten," I said.

"Really?" asked Brer Fox, staring up into the leaves.

"Oh, yes," I said.

"How do you get them?" Brer Fox asked. "That trunk is far too wide for me to climb and the branches are far too high for me to grab hold of."

"You don't have to climb the tree to get them," I said. "They come to you."

Brer Fox scratched his head. "What do you mean?"

"Patience. All you need is patience and they'll come to you." I said. "Simply sit under the tree, look up and open your mouth. They'll fall straight in."

"Are you sure?" asked Brer Fox, still very confused.

"How do you think I get them?" I asked. "I may not be able chase my food on land but I can wait for it to come to me. Just like Sister Spider and her web."

So Brer Fox sat under the tree and looked up.

"They'll only fall if you open your mouth ready to catch them," I said. "They don't like landing on the grass."

Brer Fox held his head back, opened his mouth as wide as he could and waited.

"Uck 'gis?" he asked, trying not to close his mouth.

"That's right," I said. "If you wait long enough they'll just start dropping straight into your mouth."

I watched Brer Fox for a little while, then decided it was time to go home. "Well, I must be on my way," I said. "Enjoy your plums,"

"I 'ill," said Brer Fox, still trying to keep his mouth open.

As I walked back to my pond I looked over my shoulder and he was still waiting with his mouth open, hoping those pimmerly plums would drop into his mouth.

When I was out of sight I started to laugh. I laughed so loud and for so long that by the time I got home I could hardly breathe. In fact, I had tears running down my cheeks and my jaw was beginning to ache.

"Do you know how long he sat there?" asked Brer Rabbit.

Brer Turtle smiled a large smile, then said, "I have no idea."

The two friends looked at one another and started to laugh and laugh at the thought of poor Brer Fox waiting and waiting for those pimmerly plums to drop into his mouth.

• • •

"Only a fool tests the depth of the water with both feet."

African proverb

BRER RABBIT AND THE MOON
IN THE MILLPOND

As the moon and stars glistened in the cloudless sky Brer Rabbit and Brer Turtle sat on the edge of the millpond, under the old oak tree. As they chatted, Brer Rabbit noticed the moon's reflection in the clean, still water of the millpond.

"Look at that reflection," he said. "Isn't it wonderful? You'd almost think it was the moon itself."

"My papa always said if you picked up the moon's reflection and returned it to the sky you'd find a pot gold where the reflection had been," said Brer Turtle.

Brer Rabbit looked at the moon's reflection and then at the sky.

"A pity we can still see the moon through the leaves," said Brer Rabbit. "If we couldn't, I think I'd be fooled and try catching the reflection."

"I'd love to see that," said Brer Turtle.

Brer Turtle then saw a smile on Brer Rabbit's face. Then he saw a twinkle in his eye.

"I know that look," said Brer Turtle. "What are you planning?"

"Just a little fun," said Brer Rabbit.

"Who are you going to trick?" asked Brer Turtle.

"I'm not sure yet," said Brer Rabbit. "But would you like to help?"

Brer Turtle nodded and Brer Rabbit told him his plan.

•

The next morning Brer Rabbit woke early and started putting his plan into action. He gathered together a few branches and rope, then visited Sister Squirrel.

"My dear friend," shouted Brer Rabbit to Sister Squirrel, who was busy hiding nuts for the fall. "How are you this fine day?"

"Well, thank you," said Sister Squirrel, brushing the dirt off her paws.

"I was wondering if you could help me," said Brer Rabbit. "Brer Turtle and I were sitting under the old oak tree and a gap in the leaves let the sun shine in our eyes."

"I'm sorry to hear that," said Sister Squirrel.

"I was hoping you'd be able to put these branches across the gap," said Brer Rabbit, holding up the branches he'd collected. "I'd also like to be able to move them out of the way using this rope so later we can see the moon."

"I'd be happy to," said Sister Squirrel. "You did save my good friend Sister Goose from that rascal Brer Fox."

"You're too kind," said Brer Rabbit, giving Sister Squirrel the branches and rope.

Brer Rabbit watched as she scurried up the tree and quickly put the branches across the gap. She then tied the end of the rope around the branches and threw the other end down.

"How does that look?" she called down.

"Just what we needed," said Brer Rabbit, pulling on the rope and revealing the sky above. "Thank you, I won't forget this."

"My pleasure," said Sister Squirrel. "I must go. I've just spotted a couple of lovely crunchy acorns ready for picking." And with that she was gone.

"Now to put the next part of my plan into action," said Brer Rabbit.

•

When Brer Rabbit arrived home he got out his best pen and his best paper and wrote three invitations. First he wrote to Brer Bear. It said:

My dear Brer Bear,

Knowing how you love fishing, I was hoping you'd join me for a fishing party this evening at the millpond. If you're able to join me I'll be at the pond, under the old oak tree, just as the moon and stars come out. I do hope you can make it.

With my fondness wishes,

Brer Rabbit

Brer Rabbit folded the piece of paper, popped it into an envelope and wrote in his best handwriting 'To Brer Bear.'

He then wrote the same to Brer Wolf and Brer Raccoon. Once he'd written all three invitations, Brer Rabbit delivered them.

•

That evening Brer Rabbit and Brer Turtle were sitting under the old oak tree laughing and watching the moon's reflection. As they talked they heard three voices.

"Here they come," said Brer Rabbit with a twinkle in his eye.

"I'd better hide," said Brer Turtle with a smile. And he slipped into the water and hid among the reeds just under the old oak tree.

Just as Brer Turtle disappeared among the reeds, Brer Bear, Brer Wolf and Brer Raccoon walked around the corner, all wearing their best fishing hats and carrying their best fishing rods.

"Wonderful!" said Brer Rabbit, clapping his paws together. "You've all made it. You don't know how happy this has made me."

As everyone set up their rods Brer Rabbit asked, "Can I offer anyone a blackcurrant squash? Freshly made this morning."

"Yes, please," came three replies.

So, Brer Rabbit opened his wicker basket and poured four glasses of blackcurrant squash.

As everyone sipped their drink, Brer Rabbit pointed to the moon's reflection, then at the sky. "Strange, isn't it, that the moon's reflection is in the millpond but there is no moon in the sky?" he said.

His companions looked up at the sky then back at the surface of the millpond.

"Well I never," said Brer Bear. "That's the strangest thing I've ever seen."

"I was sure I saw the moon shining down tonight," said Brer Wolf.

"Must have fallen into the millpond," said Brer Raccoon, who then laughed.

"I've heard tell it's possible for the moon to get trapped in ponds," said Brer Rabbit.

"Oh, here comes one of his tales," said Brer Bear, with a sigh.

"No, I remember my papa telling me a story about the moon and some gold," said Brer Wolf.

"Oh yes," said Brer Rabbit. "Brer Turtle was telling me the other day how his papa told him that story. He was told if you see the moon trapped in a pond and you catch it, then return it to the sky, it leaves a pot of gold as a thank you."

"Well, I think I'll have a go at that," said Brer Bear as he cast his rod and aimed for the middle of the moon's reflection.

Everyone watched as the hook flew through the air and landed on the very edge of the moon's reflection, which then rippled a little.

"Quickly!" said Brer Rabbit. "Before it gets off your hook. Flick it up into the sky."

Brer Bear flicked his rod and watched as the line and hook arched over their heads.

Everyone waited for a moment to see if the moon reappeared in the sky, but it didn't.

"What a shame," said Brer Rabbit. "It's still trapped in the pond."

"Let me have a go,' said Brer Wolf, who paddled into the water and cast his line. High above them the line and hook curved. This time the hook landed a little nearer the middle of the moon's reflection.

"Quickly!" said Brer Rabbit. "Before it gets off your hook. Flick it up into the sky."

Brer Wolf pulled on his rod, reeling in some of the line, and flicked it so it arched above their heads.

Everyone held their breath for a moment but the moon was still trapped in the pond.

"What a shame," said Brer Rabbit, shaking his head.

"I'm sure I can catch it," said Brer Raccoon.

So he had a go but, not surprisingly, the moon didn't appear back in the sky.

Brer Rabbit sighed. "What a pity. It would have been nice to get my paws on that pot of gold."

"Brer Rabbit, why don't you have a go?" said Brer Bear.

"But if you can't catch the moon, how can I?" asked Brer Rabbit. "You're all better fishermen than I am."

"You never know," said Brer Wolf.

"Go on, Brer Rabbit, have a go," said Brer Raccoon.

So Brer Rabbit picked up his rod and hopped to the edge of the millpond.

"If you insist, but if I manage to return the moon to the sky, I'm not getting my paws wet," said Brer Rabbit, "so I'll share the pot of gold with whoever gets it first."

Everyone watched as Brer Rabbit cast his line. They watched as the line arched over them and they watched as the hook landed in the middle of the moon's reflection. Brer Rabbit then flicked the line back over their heads.

Brer Turtle knew it was time to pull on the rope, so he pulled with all his might.

The animals gasped in astonishment as the moon suddenly appeared in the sky.

"Oh my!" said Brer Rabbit. "I did it."

"I'll share the pot of gold with you!" shouted Brer Bear in excitement as he dived into the millpond.

"No, I'll share it with you!" shouted Brer Wolf, diving in.

"No, I will!" shouted Brer Raccoon, diving in after them.

And Brer Rabbit and Brer Turtle watched as the three friends spent the rest of the night looking for the pot of gold.

• • •

"Fool me once, shame on you; fool me twice, shame on me."

Chinese proverb

BRER RABBIT AND BRER TURTLE

"I can't believe how hot it is," said Brer Rabbit, wiping his face with a large red spotted handkerchief. "I need a drink of fresh cool water."

So Brer Rabbit walked to the small pond by the old oak tree. Just as he rounded the corner Brer Rabbit saw Sister Goose waddling towards him.

"Well, hello, my dear friend. How are you this sun-soaked day?" asked Brer Rabbit.

"Hot and very thirsty," complained Sister Goose.

"Didn't you drink from the pond?" asked Brer Rabbit, a little surprised.

"Brer Turtle won't let anyone drink from his pond today," said Sister Goose. "Something about the sun stealing his home."

"I'm sure he'll let me. We're good friends," Brer Rabbit told her.

"Well, good luck, my friend. He's not let anyone near his pond all day," said Sister Goose as she headed to the river.

Just as Brer Rabbit reached the edge of the pond Brer Turtle's head popped out of the water.

"What is it with everyone?" he shouted. "Not only is the

sun stealing my home, but now you want to take a little more."

"Brer Turtle, my dear friend, I just want a sip of water," said Brer Rabbit, wiping his face with his large red spotted handkerchief.

"I've not let Brer Bear, Brer Raccoon or Brer Wolf drink from my pond. So why should I let you?" asked Brer Turtle.

Brer Rabbit could see Brer Turtle wasn't in a good mood, but he was annoyed his friend wouldn't let him have a drink.

"You're a brave turtle," said Brer Rabbit. "You've obviously not heard how powerful I am."

"You forget how well I know you," said Brer Turtle. "I know you just boast and trick people and you're not going to trick me."

"Are you sure I can't have a drink?" asked Brer Rabbit.

"Brer Rabbit, as I've said, Brer Bear, Brer Raccoon and Brer Wolf haven't drunk from my pond and neither will you," said Brer Turtle, who then disappeared below the water.

As Brer Rabbit made his way to the river for a much-needed drink he thought and pondered and mused. Just as he reached the riverbank he smiled one of his mischievous smiles.

"Brer Rabbit, you're a clever fellow. All I need to do is ask for a little help and Brer Turtle will soon see I'm not a rabbit he can say no to."

•

Later that day Brer Rabbit found Brer Otter resting in the shade of the reeds.

"Brer Otter, how are you?" Brer Rabbit asked.

"I'm well, thank you," replied Brer Otter, a little worried because he knew that Brer Rabbit was always up to something.

"My friend, do you remember the deal we made?" asked Brer Rabbit. "When I could ask you for help and you wouldn't ask questions?"

"I do," replied Brer Otter. "I was hoping you'd forget."

"Oh, I never forget," said Brer Rabbit. "I need your help with a small task."

"Who are you trying to trick?" asked Brer Otter.

"Now, now," Brer Rabbit said with a smile. "You agreed not to ask questions."

Brer Otter sighed and asked, "What do you want me to do?"

"Tomorrow morning, just after the sun comes up, I want you to go to Turtle's pond and pretend you're unwell," said Brer Rabbit. "When he asks you what the matter is, tell him you crossed me and I wished you to be unwell and you are."

Brer Otter shook his head. He knew he was helping Brer Rabbit trick Brer Turtle, but he'd agreed to help, no questions asked. "Is that all you want me to do?" he asked.

"That's all," said Brer Rabbit. "Now I must be on my way. Take care, my friend."

Next Brer Rabbit found Brer Heron and Brer Mink and asked them to do the same thing.

•

The next day Brer Rabbit crept down to Brer Turtle's pond and hid out of sight. Just as the sun came up Brer Rabbit saw Brer Otter limping and looking very unwell. When he reached the pond Brer Turtle's head popped out of the water.

He was just about to shout when he looked at Brer Otter, worried. "Oh, my, you do look unwell. Is there anything I can do?"

Brer Otter coughed and with a croaky voice said, "Brer Turtle, please don't worry yourself. There's nothing you can do; it's my fault."

"What do you mean?" asked Brer Turtle.

"I said no to Brer Rabbit. He asked me if I wanted to change my mind but I didn't," said Brer Otter. "Brer Rabbit wished me unwell and I am."

"Really?" asked Brer Turtle. "But Brer Rabbit just boasts about what he can do."

"That's what I believed," said Brer Otter. "But I've learned my lesson and I'll never say no to Brer Rabbit again." With that Brer Otter limped and coughed his way back to his part of the river.

As he watched from his hiding place Brer Rabbit listened and smiled. "Well done, my dear Brer Otter. I must thank you next time I see you," he said.

•

A little later, Brer Heron who was coughing and sneezing and moaning, visited Brer Turtle's pond.

When he reached the pond, Brer Turtle's head popped

out of the water. He was just about to shout when he stopped and stared at Brer Heron. "Brer Heron, are you all right? You don't look at all well."

Brer Heron sneezed. "Well, bless me!" he said. "Brer Turtle, please don't worry. It's my fault."

"What do you mean?" asked Brer Turtle.

"Yesterday I said no to Brer Rabbit. He asked me if I wanted to change my mind but I didn't," replied Brer Heron. "I'm regretting it now."

"Do you really think it's Brer Rabbit's fault?" asked Brer Turtle. "Brer Rabbit is just a trickster."

"That's what I thought," said Brer Heron. "But I've learned my lesson and I'll never say no to Brer Rabbit again. I'm off to sleep in the reeds."

Brer Heron then slowly turned around and as he walked back to the river, he coughed, sneezed and moaned.

As he watched from his hiding place Brer Rabbit listened and smiled. "Well done, my dear Brer Heron. I must thank you next time I see you."

•

Sometime later a very untidy looking Brer Mink with a patch over one eye limped to Brer Turtle's pond.

When he reached the pond Brer Turtle's head popped out of the water. He was just about to shout when he stopped and gulped. "Dear Brer Mink, what happened?"

Brer Mink slowly rubbed his head. "I've been a very silly mink and I ignored Brer Rabbit's warning. Please don't worry yourself, Brer Turtle. It's my own fault."

"What do you mean?" asked Brer Turtle.

"Yesterday I said no to Brer Rabbit. He asked me if I wanted to change my mind but I said no. I thought he was a trickster and a boaster," replied Brer Mink. "As you can see, he's not."

"This was really Brer Rabbit's fault?" asked Brer Turtle.

"Oh yes," said Brer Mink.

"Well, I hope you feel better soon," said Brer Turtle.

"Thank you," said Brer Mink, who slowly limped back to the river, wincing with every step.

As he did, Brer Rabbit smiled. "Well done, my dear Brer Mink. I must remember to thank you when we next bump into each other."

•

Brer Rabbit stayed hidden for a little while, then decided to see if his plan had worked.

As he walked to Brer Turtle's pond he whistled a happy tune.

He had just reached the water's edge when Brer Turtle's head slowly came out of the water. When he saw Brer Rabbit his eyes became wide and Brer Rabbit was sure Brer Turtle pulled his head down into the water slightly.

"Good day, my friend," said Brer Rabbit. "I'm very thirsty and I'm hoping you'll allow me to drink from your pond."

Brer Turtle didn't reply for a moment. Brer Rabbit was sure he saw Brer Turtle gulp. "Of course you can, Brer Rabbit. You know you're always welcome to drink from my pond."

Brer Rabbit smiled. "Are you sure?" he asked. "I'm sure

yesterday you said I couldn't."

"Did I?" asked Brer Turtle, pretending to look surprised. "I must have had water in my eyes and thought you were someone else."

"Well, as long as you're sure," said Brer Rabbit. He leaned forward and took a long drink of cool, clean water from poor Brer Turtle's shrinking pond.

• • •

"Thinking is the hardest work there is, which is probably the reason why so few engage in it."

Henry Ford (1863 – 1947)

BRER RABBIT, BRER FOX AND THE WHEELBARROW

Brer Rabbit watched the large snowflakes slowly drift and settle on the already snow-covered forest floor. He sighed and slowly hopped to the pantry. Although he knew it was empty he still opened the door and looked inside. "Mmm, looks like I'm going to market," he said. He reached up and took down a small round tin covered with drawings of carrot-flavored biscuits. He shook it: no rattle. So he pulled off the lid and sighed. It was empty.

"I'm going to have to sell something," he said. He looked around his burrow and sighed again. Brer Rabbit didn't like clutter, so there wasn't much to sell. Whilst he thought he gently ran his paw along the length of his ear. "I wonder what hidden treasures are in those drawers," he asked as he hopped over to a large old oak dresser.

Brer Rabbit opened the top drawer and slid the few things inside it from one side to the other. "Nothing here," he said. He opened the next drawer: the same again. However, the third drawer was full of interesting things. He rummaged and found an old fob watch he no longer used. "This may buy me a few carrots," he said, putting the fob watch to one side. He then noticed an old quill pen. "I haven't used this in a while," he said, picking it up. "Perhaps it'll get me a parsnip or two." Brer Rabbit had soon found some things to sell and popped them into a small sack.

Once he'd wrapped up against the cold, he picked up the sack, stepped outside and watched his breath as it swirled in front of him then disappeared. Just think, carrots, parsnips and a full belly! Brer Rabbit started the long trudge to market.

Brer Rabbit had just reached Market Lane when he saw Brer Fox pushing an empty wheelbarrow.

"Morning, Brer Rabbit," said Brer Fox. "What brings you out on such a cold day?"

"An empty pantry and stomach," replied Brer Rabbit.

"That makes two of us," said Brer Fox.

"Can I join you?" asked Brer Rabbit. "It'll give us time to chat."

"That'd be nice," replied Brer Fox. "It can get a little lonely this time of year with so many of our friends hibernating."

"Yes, I do miss Brer Bear, Sister Squirrel and Brer Turtle," said Brer Rabbit. "When the weather's this cold and miserable I sometimes think I'd like to join them."

As the two friends trudged through the deep snow they caught up with the little gossip there was and shared funny stories to raise their spirits. When they finally reached the market, they agreed to meet later when they'd bought what they needed and walk home together.

•

A little later Brer Rabbit and Brer Fox met up. Brer Rabbit looked at his small sack and then into Brer Fox's wheelbarrow. Brer Rabbit smiled. What a delicious stew I could make with some of that, he thought. I wonder if there's any way I can get hold of some of those tasty-looking turnips, cabbages and onions.

"You can put your sack in here if you like," said Brer Fox, pointing at his wheelbarrow.

"Thank you," said Brer Rabbit, putting his sack into it. The two friends started to trudge through the deep, crisp white snow.

"It feels a very, very long winter," moaned Fox, as the snow crunched under their feet.

"I can't believe how much snow we've had," said Brer Rabbit. "I don't think I've ever been this cold."

Just then large, fluffy snowflakes began to fall and the cold northern wind stung their faces. Brer Rabbit and Brer Fox lowered their heads and stopped talking as they continued to make their way home.

"I've lost the feeling in the ends of my ears," complained Brer Rabbit, breaking the silence.

"I think my whiskers are frozen," said Brer Fox. After a few steps he added, "I'm not sure we're going to make it home before dark."

"Paws crossed," said Brer Rabbit. "I don't want to be out in this tonight."

The friends stopped talking again and the only sound was the crunch of the snow under their feet and their slow, heavy breathing. As they made their way all Brer Rabbit could think about was the delicious-looking vegetables in Brer Fox's wheelbarrow.

When they reached the winding track that led to Brer Bear's house Brer Rabbit smiled to himself. What a clever fellow you are, he thought, as a sneaky idea began to form.

"Why don't you try and wake Brer Bear from his slumber?" suggested Brer Rabbit. "We could stay with him tonight and carry on in the morning."

"Do you think he'll let us?" asked Brer Fox, putting down the wheelbarrow and rubbing his paws together.

"It's worth a try," said Brer Rabbit. "I'll wait here and guard our things."

"I'll be as quick as I can," said Brer Fox, who then stumbled through the deep snow towards Brer Bear's house.

As he waited, Brer Rabbit looked around and saw a snow-covered bush. "That'll do," he said. "I'll have to do this quickly. I don't want Brer Fox finding out I'm tricking him."

Brer Rabbit took hold of the handles of the wheelbarrow and pushed it behind the snow-covered bush. He then grasped the first handle and wiggled it up and down.

"Oh dear, this is going to be harder than I thought," said Brer Rabbit as he wiggled the handle up and down and then side to side. He pushed down with all his might and suddenly there was a cracking sound and the handle snapped off. Brer Rabbit smiled that smile of his and broke off the other handle.

He then hopped over to a snowdrift under a fir tree and stuck the two handles into the snow. As he did a small avalanche of snow fell from the tree's branches. "Thank you," said Brer Rabbit, smiling and looking up into the tree. "Just what I needed."

A few moments later Brer Rabbit heard the crunch of Brer Fox's feet in the snow. He grabbed hold of the wheelbarrow's handles and acted as if he was pulling as hard as he could.

"Out you come," he said, as he pretended to pull on the handles.

"What happened?" asked Brer Fox, as he hurried over to Brer Rabbit.

Brer Rabbit stopped pretending to pull and turned around and shook the snow from his ears. "I was trying to find some shelter," he said, "when suddenly snow fell from the tree, covering me from head to toes and burying your wheelbarrow."

"Are you OK?" asked Brer Fox.

"I'm fine," replied Brer Rabbit. "But try as I might, I can't pull your wheelbarrow out of the snow."

"Let me have a go," said Brer Fox.

Brer Rabbit hopped out of the way and Brer Fox grabbed the handles.

"You'll have to pull hard," said Brer Rabbit. "I've tried and tried, but it just won't budge."

Brer Fox stood with his legs apart, muscles tensed, and pulled. Instantly the handles came out of the snow and Brer Fox fell back with a soft thud. He lay in the snow for a moment, stunned.

"Are you all right?" Brer Rabbit asked.

Brer Fox stared at the handles then looked up at Brer Rabbit. "My wheelbarrow," he said. "All our lovely food."

"I'm not sure what we can do," said Brer Rabbit, trying hard not to smile.

"We could dig it out," suggested Brer Fox.

"It'll be dark soon and I'm sure my ears will get frostbite if we stay and dig it out," said Brer Rabbit. "I think we'll have to come back when it stops snowing."

"You're right," said Brer Fox, with a sigh.

"I assume you couldn't get Brer Bear to open his door," said Brer Rabbit.

"No," replied Brer Fox. "All I could hear was his famous low, rumbling snore."

"I'm off then," said Brer Rabbit. "Before it gets too dark and my ears freeze."

"Take care," said Brer Fox, who quickly turned around and walked down the lane, back to his den.

"You, too," called out Brer Rabbit, watching Brer Fox disappear into the falling snow.

Once Brer Fox was out of sight Brer Rabbit retrieved the wheelbarrow from behind the snow-covered bush and pushed it home.

•

That night Brer Rabbit peeled, chopped, diced and sliced the vegetables from his bag and most from Brer Fox's wheelbarrow. This is going to be a treat, Brer Rabbit thought as he leaned over the bubbling pot and breathed in the mouth-watering smell of the stew.

Brer Rabbit found a bowl and ladled some of the steaming stew into it. He placed the bowl on the table and sat down. As he took the first spoonful of warming stew he felt a small twang of guilt. Brer Rabbit swallowed the delicious stew, looked down at it and thought, tomorrow I'll take some of this to Brer Fox. It's the right thing to do.

• • •

"A sly rabbit will have three openings in its den."

Chinese proverb

BRER RABBIT'S NEW HOME

Brer Rabbit sat in bed yawning and scratching his ears. "There's nothing better than going to bed on a full stomach," he said. "It always makes for a good night's sleep."

Brer Rabbit flung back the covers and swung his large flat feet over the edge of the bed. Splash! Brer Rabbit gasped and quickly pulled his feet back into bed. He leaned over the edge and looked down.

"What?" he asked, his reflection looking back at him. "Moldy carrots!" he said. "Where's all this water come from?"

He looked around. The floor of his bedroom was paw-deep in freezing cold water. "Oh, well, here goes," he said. Knowing how cold the water was, Brer Rabbit held his breath, closed his eyes and prepared himself as he slowly lowered his feet into the water. "Oh, that's colder than cold," he muttered. "This isn't a good start to my day."

Trying not to make too much of a splash, Brer Rabbit shuffled across his bedroom and into the front room. He looked around and noticed water seeping under his front door and trickling down the steps. He paddled through the cold water, opened the door and more water rushed in. The silvery morning light dazzled Brer Rabbit, making him blink. When his eyes got used to the bright light he saw the icicles on the trees drip, drip, dripping on to the snow, leaving dimples in the smooth white snow.

"Wilting lettuces! So that's where all this water has come from," he said. "I'll have to put something across the door to stop more water coming in."

So Brer Rabbit went outside, found a few rocks and a plank of wood. He placed them across the bottom of his door and stood back. "That should do for the time being," he said. "Now to get rid of all that water in my burrow."

Brer Rabbit carefully stepped over the plank of wood, found a large jug and bucket and started to bail the water out. "This is going to take days to dry out," he said, looking around and shaking his head. "I'll have to find somewhere to stay for a few days. But where?"

As Brer Rabbit thought he took hold of his left ear and ran his paw along it. He then did the same with his right ear. "Perhaps I could stay with Brer Bear," he said. "No, that won't work, he's still hibernating. Where else can I stay?" Brer Rabbit then smiled that smile he did when he'd come up with a clever idea. He clapped his paws together. "I know. Grandma and Grandpa's old burrow. It'll need a good clean, but at least it'll be dry."

Brer Rabbit packed a few things into his battered brown case and was soon on his way to his grandparents' old burrow. I hope it's not too dirty and dusty, he thought as he tried to avoid the many huge, cold puddles. As he rounded a corner he saw Sister Beaver, Brer Otter and Sister Raccoon, who were standing on a small bank talking.

"Morning," said Brer Rabbit. "Are you flooded out as well?"

"Yes," replied Brer Otter. "The water's so high my furniture's floating."

"My house is in a terrible mess. I'm going to have to move out for a while," said Sister Beaver, shaking her head.

"I've never seen it this bad," said Sister Raccoon. "The track to my burrow is one large puddle."

"I had to block my door and try to bail out my burrow this morning," Brer Rabbit told them. "As soon as I removed a bucketful of water, two more came in. So, I've given up and decided I'm moving into my grandparents' old burrow."

"I think I'm going to have to put up with it," said Sister Raccoon. "I can't think of anywhere to stay."

"Same here," said Brer Otter.

"Me, too," said Sister Beaver.

Brer Rabbit ran his paw along the length of his left ear, then his right. He scratched his chin and smiled that smile again. Oh, you're a clever fellow, he thought. Why spend time cleaning Grandma and Grandpa's burrow when I can get someone else to do it?

"You can all stay in with me," Brer Rabbit offered. "It's been empty since I was a kit so I'm sure we'll have to do some cleaning. But if we work together we'll be done by teatime."

"What a good idea," said Sister Raccoon. "Thank you."

"Yes, thank you," said Brer Otter and Sister Beaver.

"I warn you," said Brer Rabbit, "I have a terribly loud snore. When I used to stay with my grandparents Grandpa would joke it sounded as if I was playing his old trombone."

"You forget, Brer Rabbit, I live with the sound of water crashing against rocks," said Brer Otter. "Your snoring can't be as loud as that."

"I live near Brer Bear," said Sister Raccoon, "and he's famous for how loud his snore is. I'm sure your snore can't be louder than his."

So it was agreed the four friends would clean the old burrow together and make it their new home whilst they waited for theirs to dry out.

•

A little later the four friends were standing in the old burrow.

"It smells very damp and dusty," said Sister Raccoon, wrinkling her nose.

"Brrr … I'm sure it's colder in here than it is outside," added Sister Beaver, a shiver running down her spine.

"It'll soon warm up when the door is mended and we have a fire going," said Brer Otter. "We just need two new hinges."

"That's not a problem," said Brer Rabbit. "You get started and I'll pop back to my burrow. I'm sure I have some hinges tucked away somewhere."

When he got outside Brer Rabbit smiled and thought,

it's a pity it's going to take me so long to find those hinges. I doubt I'll be very much help with all that cleaning and mending.

As Brer Rabbit went back to his burrow to find the hinges everyone else swept the rooms, cleaned the windows and removed the spiderwebs.

"Where do you think Brer Rabbit is?" asked Sister Raccoon. "He's been gone a long time."

"I'm sure he'll be back soon," said Brer Otter.

Just then Brer Rabbit returned. "Sorry, sorry," he said. "The lane is almost impassable; the puddles have grown larger so I had to take the long way around."

"That's all right," said Brer Otter. "Did you find some hinges?"

"Yes," replied Brer Rabbit, giving them to Brer Otter.

"Perhaps you could make a nice warm fire," suggested Sister Beaver. "I couldn't find any wood and I'm still cold, even with all the cleaning I've done."

"Good idea," said Brer Rabbit. "I'll quickly gather some wood."

When he got outside Brer Rabbit smiled and thought, it's a pity it's going to take me so long to find firewood. I doubt I'll be very much help with all the cleaning and mending.

The three friends continued to work hard tidying and repairing. Soon the old front door had been rehung, the shelves straightened and the fireplace had been swept and scrubbed.

"Where do you think Brer Rabbit is?" asked Brer Otter.

"He's been a long time."

"He can't be much longer," said Sister Raccoon.

Just as they'd finished Brer Rabbit hopped in through the front door with an armful of firewood. "Sorry, sorry," he said. "Everywhere is so wet I had trouble finding dry wood. Eventually I found some near Brer Bear's. I'll soon have a lovely warm fire going and a stew bubbling in the pot."

After their evening meal, everyone was so tired they went to bed. Well, apart from Brer Rabbit. Sitting alone in the warm kitchen, he looked around, smiled and quietly said, "They've done such a fantastic job. I think I'll make this my new home." He then hopped over and picked up his grandpa's old trombone, which was sitting by the fireplace. "I hope they move out soon," he said. "If they don't, this trombone will come in very handy."

• • •

BONUS CONTENT

Whilst researching for this book I found the following two poems dating from 1896 and 1917. The first is about Brer Rabbit receiving advice from Uncle Ephe. The second has owl presiding over an argument between the animals of the wilderness.

I hope you enjoy.

UNCLE EPHE'S ADVICE TO BRER RABBIT

Keep step, Rabbit, man!
Hunter comin' quick's he can!
H'ist yo'se'f! *Don't* cross de road,
Less 'n he'll hit you fur a toad!

Up an' skip it, 'fo' t's too late!
Hoppit - lippit! Bull-frog gait!
Hoppit – lippit – lippit - hoppit!
Goodness me, why don't you stop it?

Shame on you, Mr. Ge'man Rabbit,
Ter limp along wid sech a habit!
'F you'd balumps on yo' hime-legs straight,
An' hurry wid a mannish gait,

An' tie yo' ears down onder yo' th'oat,
An' kivir yo' tail wid a cut-away coat,
Rabbit-hunters by de dozen
Would shek yo' han' an' call you cousin,

73

An' like as not, you onery sinner,
Dey'd ax' you home ter eat yo' dinner!
But don't you go, 'caze ef you do,
Dey'll set you down to rabbit-stew.

An' de shape o' dem bones an' de smell o' dat meal
'll meck you wish you was back in de fiel'.
An' ef you'd stretch yo' mouf too wide,
You know yo' ears mought come ontied;

An' when you'd jump, you couldn't fail
To show yo' little cotton tail,
An' den, 'fo' you could twis' yo' phiz,
Dey'd reconnize you who you is;

An' fo' you'd sca'cely bat yo' eye,
Dey'd have you skun an' in a pie,
Or maybe roasted on a coal,
Widout one thought about yo' soul.

So better teck ole Ephe's advice,
Des rig yo'se'f out slick an' nice,
An' tie yo' ears down, like I said,
An' hide yo' tail an' lif' yo' head.

An' when you balumps on yo' foots,
It wouldn't hurt ter put on boots.
Den walk straight up, like Mr. Man,
An' when he offer you 'is han',

Des smile, an' gi'e yo' hat a tip;
But don't you show yo' rabbit lip.
An' don't you have a word ter say,
No mo'n ter pass de time o' day.

An' ef he ax 'bout yo' affairs,
Des 'low you gwine ter hunt some hares,
An' ax 'im is he seen a jack -
An' dat 'll put 'im off de track.

Now, ef you'll foller dis advice,
Instid o' bein' et wid rice,
Ur baked in pie, ur stuffed wid sage,
You'll live ter die of nachel age.

'Sh! hush! What's dat? Was dat a gun?
Don't trimble so. An' don't you run!
Come, set heah on de lorg wid me -
Hol' down yo' ears an' cross yo' knee.

Don't run, I say. Tut - tut! He's gorn.
Right 'cross de road, as sho's you born!
Slam bang! I know'd he'd ketch a shot!
Well, one mo' rabbit fur de pot!

Originally published in *Solomon Crow's Pockets and Other Tales* by Ruth McEnery Stuart (1849 – 1917). Published by Harpers and Brothers Publishers, New York, 1896.

BRER RABBIT YOU'S DE CUTES' OF 'EM ALL

Once der was a meetin' in de wilderness,
All de critters of creation dey was dar;
Brer Rabbit, Brer 'Possum, Brer Wolf, Brer Fox,
King Lion, Mister Terrapin, Mister B'ar.
De question fu' discussion was, "Who is de bigges' man?"
Dey 'pinted ole Jedge Owl to decide;
He polished up his spectacles an' put 'em on his nose,
An' to the question slowly he replied:

"Brer Wolf am mighty cunnin',
Brer Fox am mighty sly,
Brer Terrapin an' 'Possum - kinder small;
Brer Lion's mighty vicious,
Brer B'ar he's sorter 'spicious,
Brer Rabbit, you's de cutes' of 'em all."

Dis caused a great confusion 'mongst de animals,
Ev'y critter claimed dat he had won de prize;
Dey 'sputed an' dey arg'ed, dey growled an' dey roared,
Den putty soon de dus' begin to rise.

Brer Rabbit he jes' stood aside an' urged 'em on to fight.
Brer Lion he mos' tore Brer B'ar in two;
W'en dey was all so tiahd dat dey couldn't catch der bref
Brer Rabbit he jes' grabbed de prize an' flew.

Brer Wolf am mighty cunnin',
Brer Fox am mighty sly,
Brer Terrapin an' Possum - kinder small;
Brer Lion's mighty vicious,
Brer B'ar he's sorter 'spicious,
Brer Rabbit, you's de cutes' of 'em all.

Originally published in *Fifty Years & Other Poems* by James Weldon Johnson (1871 – 1938). Published by The Cornhill Company, Boston 1917

Dear Reader

Thank you for buying and reading this book.

We hope you enjoyed this collection of Brer Rabbit stories. If you have, would you mind leaving a quick review on Amazon? As an indie publisher reviews help readers find us and our books.

Thank you from the Mad Moment Media team.

To find out about our other books please visit us at:
www.madmomentmedia.com

BIBLIOGRAPHY

The inspiration for the tales in this collection originally appeared in the following books:

Nights with Uncle Remus by Joel Chandler Harris
Houghton Mifflin Company (1881)

Solomon Crow's Christmas Pockets and Other Tales by Ruth McEnery Stuart
Harper & Brothers, New York (1896)

Uncle Remus and Brer Rabbit by Joel Chandler Harris
Frederick A. Stokes Company (1906)